Baby's First
BANK HEIST

Written by
Jim Whalley

Illustrated by
Stephen Collins

BLOOMSBURY
CHILDREN'S BOOKS
LONDON OXFORD NEW YORK NEW DELHI SYDNEY

BLOOMSBURY CHILDREN'S BOOKS
Bloomsbury Publishing Plc
50 Bedford Square, London, WC1B 3DP, UK
BLOOMSBURY, BLOOMSBURY CHILDREN'S BOOKS and the Diana logo are
trademarks of Bloomsbury Publishing Plc
First published in Great Britain by Bloomsbury Publishing Plc

Text copyright © Jim Whalley 2018
Illustrations copyright © Stephen Collins 2018

Jim Whalley and Stephen Collins have asserted their rights
under the Copyright, Designs and Patents Act, 1988, to be identified
as the Author and Illustrator of this work

A catalogue record for this book is available from the British Library

ISBN 978 1 4088 9118 6 (HB)
ISBN 978 1 4088 9119 3 (PB)
ISBN 978 1 4088 9117 9 (eBook)

1 3 5 7 9 10 8 6 4 2

Printed and bound in China by Leo Paper Products, Heshan, Guangdong
All papers used by Bloomsbury Publishing Plc are natural, recyclable products
from wood grown in well managed forests. The manufacturing processes conform
to the environmental regulations of the country of origin.

To find out more about our authors and books
visit www.bloomsbury.com and sign up for our newsletters

JW: For Fletch + Charlie, partners in crime
SC: For Frank, George + Meg, with all my love

Getaway Travel

Baby Frank loved animals
and yet he could not get
his Mum and Dad to understand
how much he'd like a pet.

It didn't matter what it was,
a dog, a cat, or rabbit,
if Frank saw fur while out on walks
he'd lunge and try to grab it.

And though each night at story time,
young Frank would always choose
books involving birds and beasts,
from ducks to kangaroos,

his parents would not change their minds.
His mum said, "You're not ready."
"AND they cost too much," said Dad.
"Be happy with your teddy."

Frank tried to think of all the ways
a pet could be obtained.
He was sure that he could steal one,
but the problem still remained . . .

of how he was supposed to find
the money he would need
to buy his new-found furry friend
its bedding, bowl and feed.

Out shopping with his mum one day,
the answer came to Frank.
"There really is no other choice –
I'll have to rob a bank."

He waited till the coast was clear,
with Mum stuck in a queue . . .

then Frank put on a bandit mask
and disappeared from view.

Past every camera,
gate and guard,

the baby
crawled unseen.

There were no bars

or laserbeams

he couldn't fit between.

Quick as a flash, he found the vault,
and scooped up all the loot.
He swiftly stuffed the notes and coins
inside his romper suit.

Then back to Mum he scarpered and sat down without a fuss.
Nobody tried to stop him as he went home on the bus.

Late that night Frank crept downstairs
and turned on the computer,
and started searching animals
to check which ones were cuter.

He knew he wanted
something small,
but not a boring mouse,
and so it was that Frank received . . .

. . . a meerkat at his house!

He snuck his pet up to his room and kept it out of sight,
and practised looking after her, to show he'd do it right.

The meerkat was a great success, and little Frank adored it . . .

but pretty soon he wanted more – why not? He could afford it.

First a dog, and then a pig, two aardvarks and a cat
were smuggled up into his room. He should have stopped at that.

There were leopards in his cupboards and a beaver in the bath.

And Frank was **really** struggling to hide his new giraffe.

It all went wrong one afternoon
when Mum called out and said,
"Don't be alarmed
but I just found . . .

. . . a **rhino** in our shed."

It took her some detective work
to find out Frank's deceit . . .

banknotes and a bandit mask –
a pile of named receipts.

Mum showed her clues to Dad
and said it was her firm belief,
"Our baby wanted pets so
much he's turned into . . .

a thief!"

Once Frank could see how sad they were he quickly understood that stealing things was very wrong. From now on he'd be good.

Frank's parents took him to the bank and told them of the theft. The bank asked for their money but there wasn't any left.

The family went home to their pets
and wondered what to do.

Until at last Dad had a thought . . .

By selling tickets at the door they soon began to save.
Frank tried his best to lend a hand and show he could behave.

He served his time without a doubt and though still on all fours,
it didn't stop him mucking out and even leading tours.

At night he'd lie down with his pets
and gaze up at the stars.

Baby Frank had
got his way . . .

He was happy **behind bars.**